# The Efil Brothers

by Collin Lee

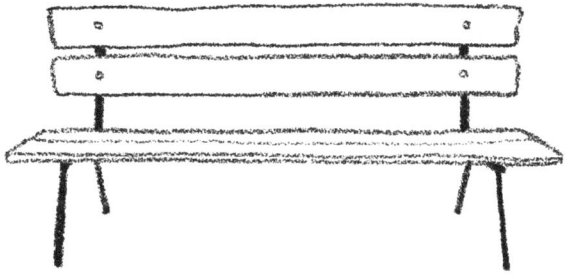

illustrated by Jiyoung Choi

Dedicated to my amazing family - Sunny, Colleen and Grant.

THE EFIL BROTHERS
By Collin Lee

Copyright © 2017 by Collin Lee
All rights reserved. No part of this book may be used or reproduced in any manner whatsoever without the written permission of Collin Lee.

ISBN: 978-0-692-82896-0

Cover design and illustrations by Jiyoung Choi

For more information, visit www.TheEfilBrothers.com

FIRST EDITION

What if you could give the gift of time?

Felix and Maurice Efil, twin brothers, lived in Nowhereville.
 Everybody knew them, but nobody knew how long they'd been around.
 It seemed like forever.
 Felix owned a small watch shop.
 And Maurice owned the mortuary next door.

Every morning, they sat on the bench in front of the shop,
sipping coffee and waiting for Pierre, the paperboy.
At first, they would hear the familiar creaking of an old bicycle in the distance,
as if to awaken all the slumbering souls in town.
Then they would see the scrawny ten-year-old boy on his old rusty bicycle,
smiling in the wind.

But lately, the sound of the bicycle seemed weaker,
and he seemed scrawnier.

Pierre would pull up next to the Efil Brothers,
greet them warmly and hand them their fresh newspapers.
Then he would go over to the watch shop window, admiring all those watches,
especially the old dusty pocket watch that sat in the corner.
Something about it – perhaps the engraving of a knight slaying
a dragon on the cover – drew him in.
Then Felix would walk up to him, put his hand on Pierre's small shoulder
and ask for the thousandth time, "How does it look today?"
The answer was always the same,
"It looks even better today. Someday, it'll be mine."
"Of course, it will. Of course," Felix would say with a gentle squeeze of his
frail hand, and Pierre would look up at his kind eyes.
It was another beautiful morning.

One day, as Pierre was about to get back on his bicycle after his daily ritual
in front of Felix's shop, a large black sedan almost ran him over.
It belonged to Mr. Blanc, the richest man – yet the stingiest,
as they sometimes are – in town.
He was a very tall, pale and obese man.
He stepped out of his sedan and walked straight into Felix's shop.

Inside the shop, Mr. Blanc browsed through
the watches on display.
"How come none of them are working?" asked Mr. Blanc.
"Because they are all hand-wound, sir. The best kind,"
answered Felix.
After a moment of browsing, Mr. Blanc picked up a gold one
with diamond markers and looked at it carefully.
It was a beautiful watch.
The watch face had two small windows, showing a month
and a date, a week from that day.
The hands pointed to noon.
And on the back was a peculiar four-digit number engraved on it,
perhaps indicating a calendar year?
If it were, it was that very year.
"I'll take this one," said Mr. Blanc and handed it to Felix.
As soon as Felix touched the watch, it began to tick magically.

After his expensive purchase, Mr. Blanc's sedan pulled away.
Felix came over to the bench and sat down next to Maurice
who was still enjoying his morning coffee.
"He bought one," said Felix.
"I see," Maurice answered.
"The gold one with diamond markers," Felix added.
Then the Efil Brothers simply sat there for a long time, enjoying the morning sun.

That afternoon, although there was no phone call or a visit,
Maurice began preparing a peculiarly large casket.
He knew it would take about a week.

For the next three days, Pierre's bicycle sounded weaker and weaker,
and his smile got smaller and smaller.
Then on the fourth day, there was no sign of him.
The morning was quiet, too quiet.

About ten miles away was Pierre's home.
It was not much more than a small room, so not much was needed,
and not much was there.
Pierre laid in the only bed in the room, stricken with fever.
His mother sat next to him, holding his hand helplessly.
She looked pale and older than she was.
Those wrinkles on her face weren't from aging but from suffering.

With her hollow eyes fixed on her only child, she began to sing quietly,

"When I held you for the first time,
My life finally became life.

When I held you for the thousandth time,
My life was so much more.

You gave me so much,
But I could only give you so little.

When my heart was empty,
You filled it with love.

But the only thing I can do now,
Is fill your heart,

With this quiet song...."

Just the day before, she had received a phone call
from the nearby hospital.
It was about Pierre.
When she hung up the phone, the only thing she could do
was blankly look up at the mold-infested ceiling.
What she felt was beyond sadness that no tear could wash away.
But he's my only child,
those words echoed in her heart until it shattered to pieces.

A week had passed, and the church bell in the distance announced the time, noon.
Maurice, dressed in a black suit, came into his office
and sat down behind a small oak desk.
His eyes seemed to be waiting for a phone call.
Moments later, it rang.
It was the local police.

The funeral itself was quite grandiose.
But the mourners were few and far between.
To those few who came to pay their last respects,
Mr. Blanc was still the richest in town.
But alas, he couldn't even afford an extra breath of life.

The next morning was even colder.
But the Efil Brothers thought they heard something in the distance
that warmed their hearts.
It was the familiar rhythmic creaking of their little friend's rusty bicycle.

When the distant figure took shape before their eyes,
the Efil Brothers were surprised.
It wasn't Pierre.
But her eyes were unmistakably his – or rather, his were hers.

She pulled over to the side, rested the bicycle against the lamppost, and walked into Felix's shop.
Felix followed.

"May I help you?" asked Felix.
She looked up at him with eyes drowned in sorrow.
He nodded as if he understood what her eyes said and gently uttered,
"Please, take your time and have a look."
For a moment, in the stillness of the air,
she gazed at the rows of watches in front of her.
Then her weak voice broke the silence,
"Sir…can I trade the bicycle outside for a watch? I can pay you
the balance in two weeks. You see, I have a sick boy at home, and he…."
Tears flooded her words.
"I can do better," replied Felix,
"You can choose any watch you'd like, and it's on me."
Despite the tears, she stared at him.
Really? Why?
"Pierre is a good boy. He loves his mother."

She didn't know what to say, but she also knew no word was needed.
He understood.
Her mind began to race.
Any watch?
Even the gold one?
If I sell it, perhaps the doctors can find a way.
But I can't take it.
It's too expensive.
But he said any watch....

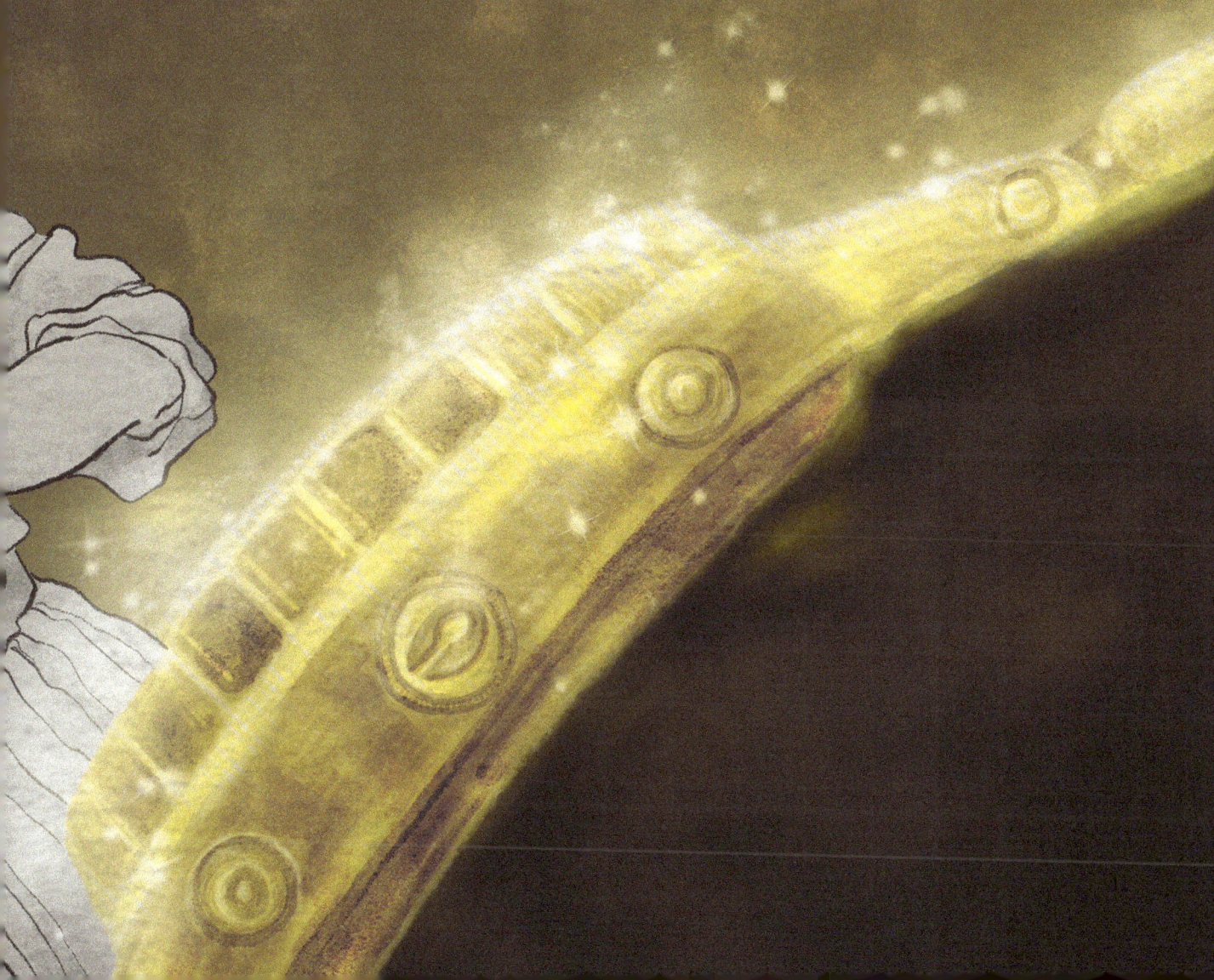

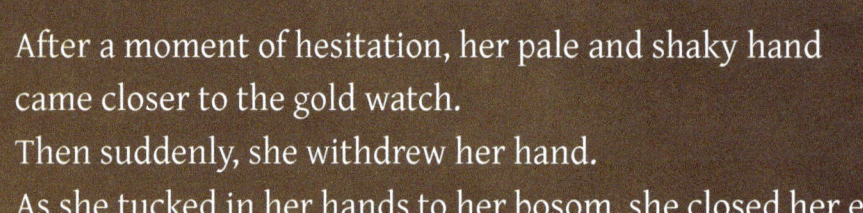

After a moment of hesitation, her pale and shaky hand
came closer to the gold watch.
Then suddenly, she withdrew her hand.
As she tucked in her hands to her bosom, she closed her eyes.
She couldn't decide.
She remembered her son excitedly talking – often – about a pocket watch
with an engraving of a knight slaying a dragon.

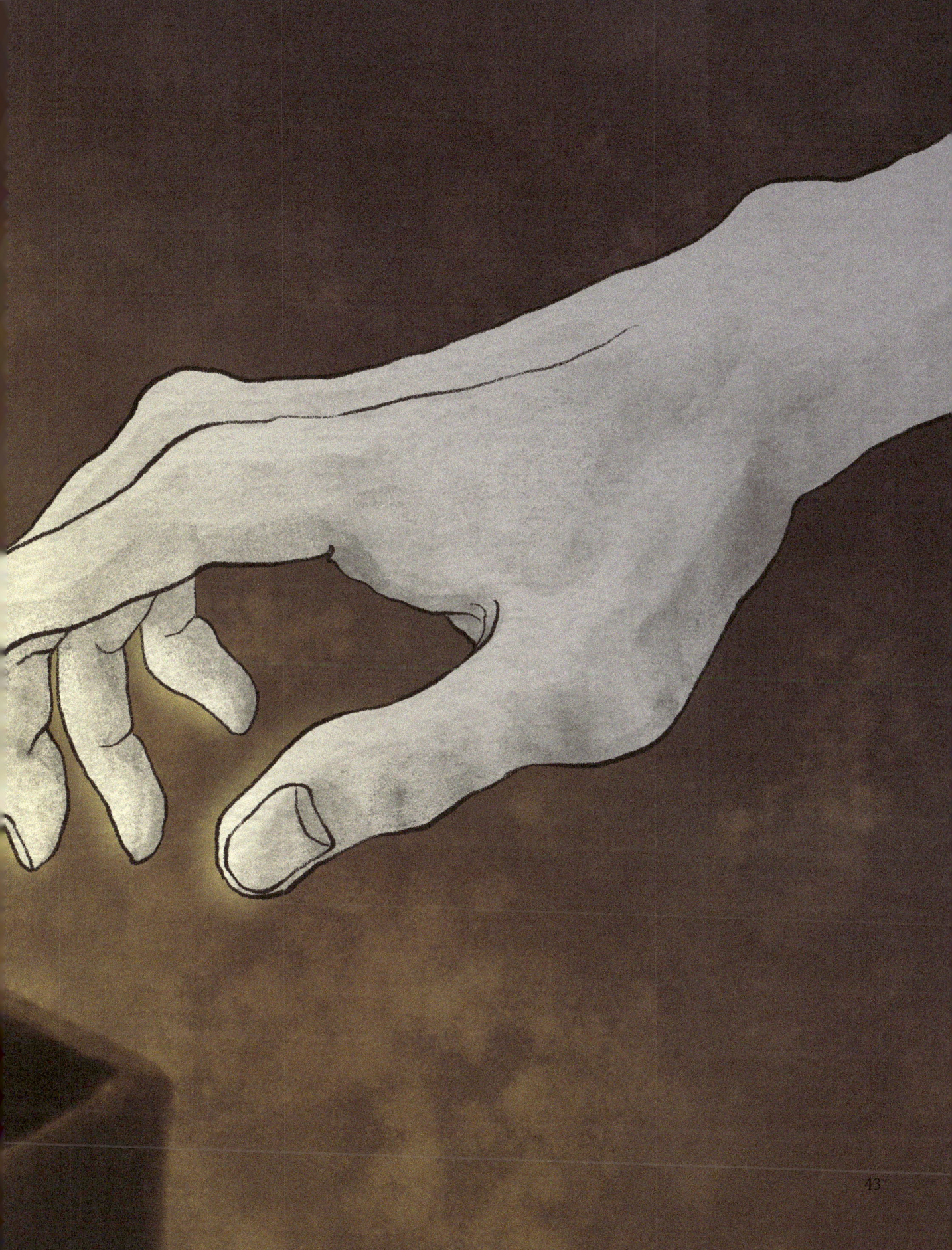

Stepping over to the corner, she looked at the familiar – although
she'd never seen it before – pocket watch covered with dust.
She touched it gently, and dust floated into the air, like a magical puff of smoke.
She knew what she had to do.

She turned and picked up the gold one.
The watch unmistakably had two small windows,
showing a month and a date, that very day.
And the shiny gold hands pointed straight up, to midnight.
When she turned it over, the back had a four-digit number
that coincided with that year.

After thanking Felix heartily, she rushed out of the shop and headed down the street.
"Well?" asked Maurice, still sitting on the bench.
"It's...the gold one." Felix's words felt final.
Maurice dropped his head.

That afternoon, when Felix visited Maurice at the mortuary,
he saw a small casket being prepared.
Maurice didn't want to admit it, but he knew he didn't have much time.

At the diner down the street, Pierre's mother was waiting tables.
But her mind was on the one-and-only thing in her pocket, the gold watch.
Tired from work, she wiped her forehead and looked out at the street.
Just for a split second, she thought she saw Pierre riding his bicycle to Felix's shop.
Suddenly she felt an ache in her heart.

The night was falling in Nowhereville.
The lampposts dotted the foggy air.
Felix turned off the lights in his shop and turned the sign on the door to "Closed."
As he stepped out, he saw Pierre's bicycle, still leaning against the lamppost. It looked lonely.

He took a deep breath of the chilly air and was about to head out
when he heard footsteps, someone running toward him.
The person's silhouette emerged from the fog and approached him.
When the lamppost finally sprinkled light on the person,
he knew he had to reopen the shop.

Inside the shop, a familiar hand was touching the dusty
pocket watch in the corner, almost caressing it.
Then a familiar female voice – still weak but more at peace – whispered,
"He'd love it."
The hand picked up the pocket watch and opened the cover.
It showed midnight on Christmas.
The hand turned it over,
and the back unmistakably had a four-digit number….

She waved goodnight at Felix who stood by the door,
got on the bicycle and rode into the night,
leaving behind the familiar creaks that cut through the sheets of foggy air.

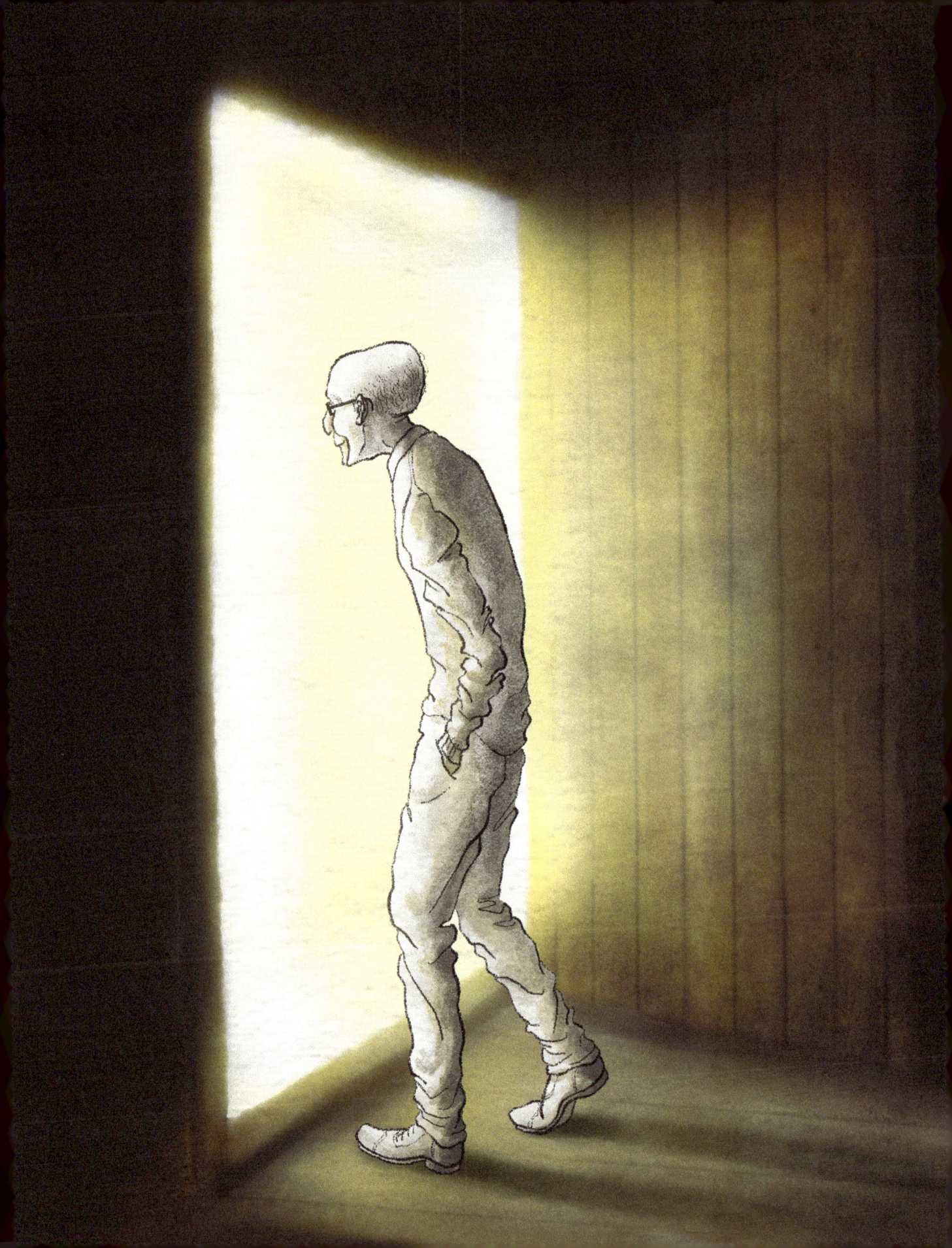

Felix opened the door to Maurice's workshop at the mortuary.
The small casket was almost done.
"She came back," Felix said.
"And?"
Felix simply nodded.
A thin smile blossomed on Maurice's wrinkled face.

The Elfi Brothers sat in front of the fireplace at the mortuary office.
They would stay up all night since they had – unexpectedly –
plenty of wood from the workshop.
The night was long, but it was peaceful.

The next morning came, as Time always delivers.
As they have been for who-knows-how-long, the Efil Brothers sat by the bench, sipping coffee and enjoying the morning sun.
Then they thought they heard what they had been waiting for all night.
Yes, this time, the creaking of the rusty bicycle sounded stronger than ever....

 The End

CPSIA information can be obtained
at www.ICGtesting.com
Printed in the USA
LVHW07*1419120318
569548LV00023B/521/P

9 780692 828960